D0257686

HODDER CHILDREN'S BOOKS
First published in Great Britain in 2017 by Hodder and Stoughton

Text copyright © Peter Bently, 2017
Illustrations copyright © Garry Parsons, 2017

A CIP catalogue record for this book is available from the British Library.

HB ISBN: 9781 444 92853 2
PB ISBN: 9781 444 92854 9

10 9 8 7 6 5 4 3 2 1

Printed and bound in China

Hodder Children's Books
An imprint of Hachette Children's Group
Part of Hodder and Stoughton
Carmelite House
50 Victoria Embankment
London EC4Y 0DZ

An Hachette UK Company
www.hachette.co.uk
www.hachettechildrens.co.uk

FSC
www.fsc.org
MIX
Paper from
responsible sources
FSC® C104740

PETER BENTLY & GARRY PARSONS

The Tooth Fairy's Royal Visit

Hodder Children's Books

The Tooth Fairy woke
from her afternoon nap
when Robin arrived
in a bit of a flap.

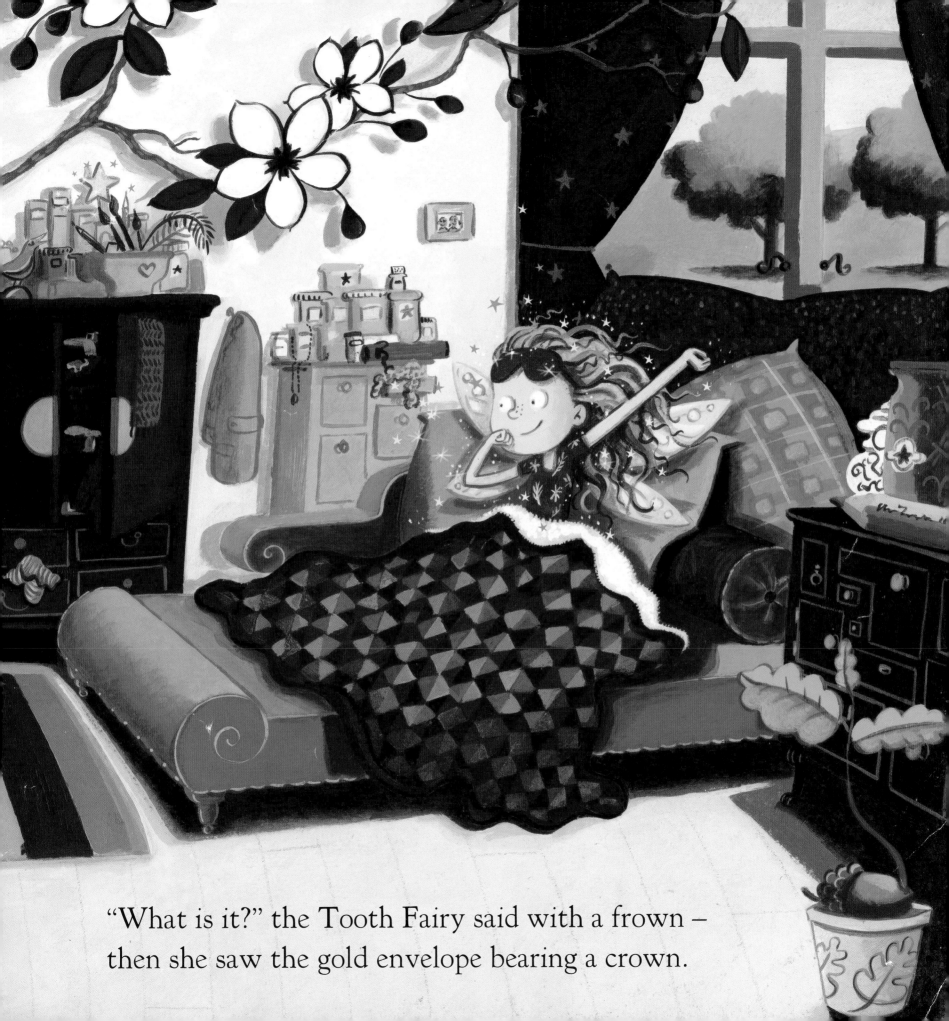

"What is it?" the Tooth Fairy said with a frown –
then she saw the gold envelope bearing a crown.

She opened the letter and giggled with glee.
"Oh-ho! It's a trip to the palace for me!

Dear Tooth Fairy,
Her Majesty the Queen is pleased to inform you that her royal great-grandson has lost his first tooth.
You will find it under his pillow tonight.
Yours Sincerely,
The Queen
xx

The prince lost his very
first tooth today.

As soon as it's night-time
I'll be on my way."

That night, at the palace,
the lights were all out.
"Good," thought the Tooth Fairy.
"No one's about."

She flew over the railings but got a big fright...

when
FLASH!
– she set off the
security light!

Dazzled and blinking,

she shot through the yard –

and flew with a WALLOP straight into a guard!

"Yikes!" he declared,
as she bounced off his hat.
"Whatever was that?
A small owl? Or a bat?"

The Tooth Fairy whizzed round the palace and sighed.
There was no way to enter, as hard as she tried.

And then – a door opened! She dashed for the gap –

as three
little corgis
ran out –

Yap!
Yap!
Yap!

They snapped at her heels
and knocked over a bin. . .

with a CLATTER and CRASH!
What a terrible din!

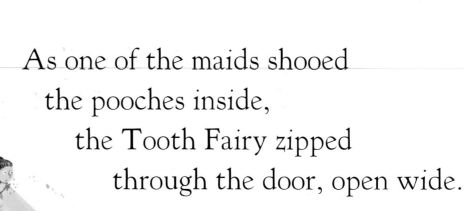

As one of the maids shooed
the pooches inside,
the Tooth Fairy zipped
through the door, open wide.

The maid cried,
"Oh bother!
I've let in a moth!"

And she gave the poor fairy
a flick with her cloth!

She fell on some knickers marked
'HM The Queen' –

and **nearly** got put
in the washing machine!

The Tooth Fairy fled
through a splendid great hall
where cleaners were
clearing up after a ball.

"This palace is huge!"
she declared. "Goodness me!
Now, where on earth can
the little prince be?"

She flew here,

she flew there.

Then she saw, from afar,

light from a door

that was slightly ajar.

"Aha!" said the fairy.
She peeped round the door...
and saw an old lady,
crouched down on the floor!

"I can't find my dentures!" the old lady frowned.
"Where have I put them? I've looked all around."

The Tooth Fairy smiled.
"Let me try a quick spell.
I find that it normally
works very well...

Oh dentures!
Oh dentures!
Oh, where can you be?
Come to me, come to me!
FIBBLE-DE-FEE!"

A pillow rose upwards and there, underneath,
clacking away – was a set of false teeth!

The lady said, "Thank you!" and popped her teeth back. "Now, would you care for a small bedtime snack?"

But the fairy said, "Sorry, I'm all in a tizz. I need to find out where the little prince is!"

"The prince?" smiled the lady. "Why didn't you say?
Come, little fairy. He's not far away."

The tooth was soon found,
a coin left in its place –
and the Tooth Fairy saw
a familiar face.

"Thank you, dear fairy,"
the old lady said.
"Now please let me help you
get home to your bed."

The Tooth Fairy gave a great gasp of delight
when she saw what was taking her homewards that night –

a fine golden carriage,
the grandest she'd seen.
"Goodnight!" said the fairy.

"Goodnight!" said...

the Queen!